Peanut Butter Patty

Kyra Dacanay Perry

ISBN: 1-4392-2662-8
ISBN-13: 9781439226629

Visit www.peanutbutterpatty.com to order additional copies.

This book
is dedicated
to
my grandmothers

Rosalinda G. Dacanay
Miriam B. Perry

Special thanks to
my teachers
who helped and encouraged me:
Julie Massey
Jane Schwefler
Patricia Merry
Joi Kilpatrick
Nancy Mason

Prologue

I've always heard people say things like "Shoot for the stars" or "Follow your dreams". But of course, grownups are supposed to say things like that. Once I finally got my shattered dreams pieced back together, I figured out that fairy tales aren't just where you find happy endings. But you find them in everyday things that you do. Life is just like a sea. One day you're swimming and the next day you're sinking. So I guess now, I figured out that wherever you go, there will be an angel watching you oh so closely. Life's current will carry you far. But it is better to go with it and away from all you've known than to fight it. I had fought it so much that life had become absolutely miserable. But once I figured out just to let the world have a few shots at me and then bounce back and show everyone you're bigger and better than that. So everyone's life is a learning experience.

\

Chapter I

The sun was beating down, on what seemed to be directly on me. I was sitting on the school playground's hot black steps. I was thinking....just thinking.

All the girls in the class were formed into an ovalish circle. They were chanting "Sally Walker". I just watched, never liking to be the center of attention.

The sun made a watery line, which made everything look melted. The hot sun stung my arms and turned them a hint of pink.

It was all changing. Then it started.

We made our way down the tiled halls back to our homeroom class. I saw Kim (my "best" friend) talking to the movie star wannabes.

She was laughing at me. No one cared anymore though - not me, not Kim, and not the populars.

It was all getting pretty old. I grabbed my old beat up backpack, and brought it to my desk to pack my things up.

But then Kim walked by with a face full of excitement and craziness. She dug her long, dirty nails into my backpack and threw it to the floor. I gave a sort of annoyed grunt and picked it up from the floor.

I waited until the third bell rang. When it finally did, I scampered down the hall in a half jog. I started the two block journey down the Route 12 sidewalk. My jog became faster and faster until the wind sent my hair thrashing at my face, and a harsh howling through my ears.

All got quiet when I turned down Berry Lane.

Mrs. White, sitting on her porch like always, let out a little grin. She tried to hide the fact that she was very lonely. I let out a waving hand back.

I slid down my gravel driveway and flung open the door. I slung my backpack to the wood floor, grabbed my reading book and pulled a batch of cookies out of the chilly fridge.

I trotted over to Mrs. White's small and compact, little white house. Yellow daisies lined the brick steps that led to two wickers chairs, one with Mrs. White in it. She was dressed in an old pink and black flowered dress. It made her hazel eyes really stand out.

"Hi Mrs. W, I've come to read to you," I smiled and slunk into the empty chair.

"My, my, let me pour you a cup full of lemonade while I listen to the best reader across the seas!" She reached for the pitcher and poured lemonade into two ice filled glasses.

"Oh, Mrs. W. Have a cookie. It's your favorite." She took the cookie as I started reading "The Great Gilly Hopkins". Mrs. W's favorite book. I must have read it about seven times.

At 7:28 pm she fell asleep. I lugged her in the wheelchair to a bedroom full of antiques. I got to my house five minutes later. Mom had just set the table and smiled her pageant winning smile.

We sat down and Maggie, our dog, was scraping at the table legs. She decided to scrape mine, which left an ashy trail.

Mag sat on her tail and pouted, so I "accidentally" dropped some mashed potatoes on the ground. I washed my plate and climbed the squeaky old stairs to my worn wood bed, threw the green sheets over my head, and fell asleep thinking.

Chapter 2

In the morning, the sun was still out, the birds still chirping, and the leaves still green. It was all the same.

I walked my usual route to school. *Someone* must have forgotten that they had an issue with me. But instead, everywhere I went people would attempt to trip me and most succeeded. Then Kim approached me on the way to the restroom and slid her pink shoe at me unexpectedly and I came crashing.

Recess was the same except this time I tried jumping rope. It was fine until someone would walk by and step on the rope.

When we headed back to the building, the first thing that happened was I went soaring through the air and landed pressed against the yellow tiles.

Today I didn't, couldn't, wait til the third bell rang. Instead, I left at the first. I took the same way, but this time I was running faster, and my heart was pounding harder than usual.

Until, of course, I turned down Berry Lane.

Mrs. W was looking ill and tired. I didn't even stop by my house to drop my stuff off. I ran up the narrow steps to her porch.

"You ok, Mrs. W?" I asked worriedly.

"Oh, you know when you get old, nerves get to you," she replied faintly.

"Would you like me to put you in the bed?" I started wheeling her inside before she could answer.

"That'd be fine, but could you still read?" she asked.

"Yes," I replied as I guided her to her wood bed painted white and tucked her under her flowered sheets.

Right as I cracked my book open, I heard a tender snore. I grabbed my stuff and made a straight line for the door.

6

I slid across the driveway, hitting the gray asphalt and scraping my leg, making a thin layer of skin rip off my knee. It was fine. Nothin' like another scrape to go with the other five.

Noodles were boiling on the stove at home. Guess we're having meat sauce spaghetti.

As the back door slammed shut Mom grabbed her chest and squalled, "Good heavens, Maly!"

Once she figured out it was me, she just talked her normal way. "Why are you here so early darling? Is everything alright?" she asked.

"Yes Ma'm. Mrs. W fell asleep after a long hard day," I replied.

"Oh, well is that right Maly?" she questioned half listening.

"Yes Ma'm," I answered.

"Help with supper would you hun?" Mom yelled back from the pantry.

"Sure," I grabbed a fork and started jabbing the little slimy noodles in the pot.

The steam was making the hot late spring day seem like not only the noodles were boiling but me too.

Mom came back with the Hunt's spaghetti meat sauce and poured it over the noodles I had just scooped into a big bowl. It made a thick blanket of steam rise up. As I dropped the fork into the boiling pot, more water than usual splatted out of the pot towards my face. I was dodging water drops left and right until one hit me right between the eyes.

I reacted by grabbing my sore face in my warm sweaty hands.

Mom cried, "Honey, what did YOU do?"

"I'm fine," I replied uncovering my burnt face.

"Ok, then if you're fine, set the table, usual spots," Mom smiled knowing if she made a fuss about it I would too.

"Ok"

"Thanks my Peanut Butter Patty."

I laid out three clear plates and took some tongs out to the table to serve the slimy slithers of spaghetti.

Mag came in, her toenails tapping against the wood floor. She pawed at her food bowl, in a "I'm hungry, feed me" way. I poured out the little round pieces of kibble and the cool splashing water.

I was tempted to stick my burning face into the cold water bowl until a saw a dead fly in it.

Chapter 2

Mag lapped up all of her water and chowed down all of her food, while we were "enjoying" our food. This time not in silence.

Dad kept blabbing on and on about his day and Mom was asking a thousand questions about the spaghetti. They were both trying to blast the other. In no time their faces were red and they were looking at me like I could understand both of them at the same time.

I did what worked best, agreed and nodded. After supper Dad and Mom made me do all the dishes. I blew bubbles out of the soap container. I didn't care what I did.

It was Friday night, and the moon was low in the sky. It was like the moon got closer and closer every day. I decided to catch some rest for the morning time, when I fix Mrs. W her breakfast.

Chapter 3

My little heavy aluminum clock rang so hard and loud it almost fell off my small wobbly night stand. Sitting next to my clock was a tall dusty lamp. It was black at the stem and at the top a polka-dotted shade.

Mrs. W wakes up at 7:30 am sharp every day, no exceptions. So that means I have to be up by at least 6:45 am.

I turned on the cold metal shower head and felt the water until it was the perfect temperature. Every time I first stepped in, I'd get a shiver up and down my back, and lumpy goose bumps up my arms and legs. The quiet shower was the only place where I could do my best thinking; listening to the drops of water hitting the bare white floor, echoing off the side of the walls. The hot stuffy air that filled the small room was relaxing and calming.

When I got out after twenty minutes, I twirled my hair up in a towel bee hive which towered over my head. I brushed my teeth with my hard, stiff toothbrush and combed my hair out, unknotting all the clumps of hair. I threw on some old basketball shorts and a loose shirt (that I think was my Mom's, but she got mixed up and put it in my drawer). That put me at 7:20 am. I threw on my holey socks, and my dirty Converses.

I was just stomping up the red brick stairs when I saw Mrs. W's bedroom light flicker on as always. I helped her out of bed and greeted her with, "Hi, good Saturday morning!'

She didn't reply, just groaned and muttered.

I plopped her in her wheelchair, and rolled all 152 pounds into the kitchen. I whipped up some buttermilk biscuits and poured her a glass of O.J. She wouldn't eat until I sat down and prayed. She was a Southern, front row, church person. I, on the other hand, sat in the third row and sometimes peeked during prayer.

———

I started, "Thank you Lord for this day, and this food, Amen."

"Thank you," Mrs. W managed to get out through all the biscuits in her mouth, which was one.

I looked around the same room I looked at every Saturday. But this time, I really saw it. All the memories spilling over and out the tiny cracks in the walls. All the pictures in place, like a scene in little movies; some happy, ending with smiles, some ending with tears.

I took up the plate after she was finished and washed them with her lavender soap, drying them with her daisy flower towels.

I left her sitting in her favorite spot, the first wicker chair to the right. She held a cup of tea in hand and paper in the other. I always wondered about what she was writing. She only wrote when the wind was calm, all quiet, and all alone on her little old porch.

But the times when I was there, she would let me draw the little finches living in the corner of the porch. I only drew for her. No one knew, except for her. But on the rare occasion I did draw for her she brought me parchment paper and a perfectly pointed pencil.

She thought the world of my drawings, calling them "talent on paper". She said that each of us has a bird inside, waiting till the right time to fly, soar and SHINE.

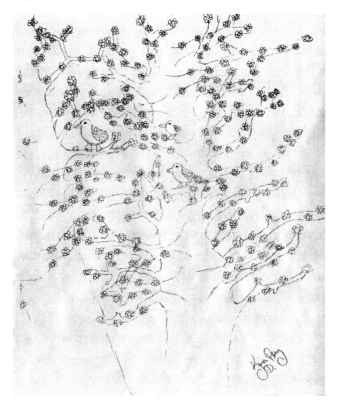

When I got back home, Dad was gone and Mom was doing some dusting with her rainbow colored feather duster.

I noticed that she had her "cleaning Mom" face on so I took a broom and "made myself useful."

On the bar was a sealed note that looked important. Beside her were two cases of luggage.

Wow, we've only gone on two vacation trips, to Florida and Virginia. But judging by the amount of stuff in these suitcases it looked like we were moving.

She didn't notice I was sweeping, or even that I was there. So I put the broom back and went to my bed.

———

Chapter 4

Soon Mom came in, but I didn't know because I was fast asleep, running a high fever.

I slowly opened my eyes. The wall was spinning and Mom's head above mine was circling. She whispered, "Babe, it'll be alright. Put this under your tongue."

She shoved a thermometer into my face. I barely had enough strength in my jaw to open my mouth. The numbers kept getting higher and higher until finally it reached the number 102.5. I was 2.5 degrees under overheating.

She exclaimed, "Oh my!" She dashed to the kitchen sink for a cold water towel.

I got goose bumps and finally got enough energy to squeak out, "I - I'm coo- cold."

"Oh Babe, let me grab you three blankets."

I laid in bed all of that day. I didn't even leave my room to go to supper. It was brought to me.

When my door was left open for just a minute I glimpsed out into the hall and noticed the luggage wasn't there. Good to know we were staying right where we were — down Berry Lane.

I floated off into a dream I couldn't quite remember. Something that was like "Leave it to Maly" instead of " Leave it to Beaver." Always making a goof and messing up practically everything.

I slept til noon the next day. I woke up when I heard my parents' car pull up in the driveway, grinding the gravel under their tires.

Mom came in and said, "We missed you at church today. They even put you on the prayer list. Are you hungry? Thirsty? Hot? Cold?"

I heard my stomach growl at the sound of food. Mom came up with a plate of home-made biscuits and chocolate milk. I saw the dark chocolate spots swirling in my cup. They stuck to the bottom of the cup after I drank it all down.

My fever slowly got low enough for me to go to school on Wednesday. When I got there all I could think about was everything. Everything, but nothing. I was reading a lot of books by the time I got better. Three counting "The Great Gilly Hopkins."

The day was still usual, until the third bell rang. I suddenly felt anxious inside the pit of my stomach as I dashed across the hard cement to Berry Lane.

Mrs. W was not on the porch. She wasn't there all week. Maybe she was lonely, or maybe she was sick. I walked up her steps. I was nervous. What if, if.... I beat on the door. It thumped. I turned the knob. Her bedroom door was open.

"Mrs. W , are you okay?" I screamed at the top of my lungs.

"Y-yue - yes child," she was able to stutter out. She slid the paper halfway under her lopsided mattress as I ran in. She strained to get up until I grabbed her soft, vein filled arms and pulled her back on the bed.

"Don't get up. Have you eaten? No?" I replied for her. "What-cha like? Fried Taters?" I asked with a smile, relieved that she was alright.

I walked to the kitchen and pulled out the brown potatoes. I peeled and fried them until they were crisp, a hint of brown and a bit of flakes. Just how Mrs. W liked them.

I put them on a purple plate with ketchup on the right side of it. It was so hot the steam burnt the air, so I had to blow it off for her.

She fell asleep with the plate in her hand. I put it on her side table, just in case, and left.

———

Chapter 5

I started walking home, but I kept hearing things. Rattles, psssst, and other weird noises coming from behind a few trees. I cautiously walked toward the noise and around the tree.

There she was, a girl, slumped down at the roots of the tree. She was in a pink Sunday dress and brown flats, straight blonde hair. Me, on the other hand, wore casual clothes, practical tennis shoes, black hair with brown highlights in tight fresh curls tied with a blue ribbon.

She stared with squinty eyes and finally said, "Kate, you?"

I guessed that was her name, she didn't say it too well. Afraid to use my real name I said, "Peanut Butter Patty."

She gave a chuckle, "Really?"

"That's what you can call me," I replied in a stern manner.

"Fine. I've been hiding out here for two hours," Kate stated matter-of-factly.

"Why?" I asked wanting to know more about this strange girl.

"I ran away, my....Well, anyway I'm here now - and starving," she complained.

"Oh," I said softly. I was thinking she can't go to my house..... Maybe Mrs. W.....

"You can stay with my neighbor, only if you're like invisible," I offered.

"Who's that?" Kate perked up when she thought her luck may be turning for the better.

"Mrs. White. She is sort of old," I explained. "But if you stay there you have to wait on her and get her things.....Deal?"

Kate thought for a long moment and blurted, "I like you Peanut Butter Patty, so . . . sure."

I walked back with Kate to Mrs. W's house and she was awake. I told her the plan but I wondered if - what - would happen.

She was glad and exclaimed, "Oh, I've always wanted a daughter!"

Kate seemed to back away a bit at the thought of her, a daughter. But to me, it was settled.

I put sheets in the guest room and toasted some bread with butter for Kate. After that, I left them both and headed for my house.

The sun was setting in the horizon, the breeze was picking up. The sun was electric orange with purple clouds playing around it.

When I walked through the door my parents' attention shifted from their food to me.

"You're late," stated my Dad. "Sit down and eat your food. Why are you late?"

"Ummm, Mrs. W kept me late," I said slowly and partly lying. I pulled out the heavy wood chair, sat down and ate the salad in front of me.

Later, in bed, I kept wondering - will they be okay? What will happen? Did I make a good choice? I kept turning in bed hearing little voices in my head, like you do when you're half thinking out loud and half asleep.

Chapter 6

I jumped up when the alarm from my clock began to ring. My pjs stuck to my skin from the sweat. It was the last day of school.... Here comes summer, I guess.

For this rare day I put on my usual. It's still school. The first thing I did was tie my tightly curled hair up in my usual blue ribbon.

The things I love about me are my hair and my slim, fit body. I actually have the body of a model - except with scrapes up and down my legs. I refuse to wear dresses (except for funerals and church). And I didn't believe in covering my face with that lumpy gunk called make-up. I liked me, like me.

I walked this time to school. I didn't care if I was late. It was May 23, the date of, well, of almost summer, I guess. Like we'd learn anything important anyway. The teachers would be rejoicing over no more of these "littles" (that means students) that make their lives so much harder. I didn't think it was even hard to begin with.

I got to school forty-five minutes late. They didn't care. The pops (populars) were in the front four seats with Kim next to the most popular pop. Blue eyed, blonde hair flipped to perfection, Tiffany Joans in her pink dress outfit.

I decided to stay away from them and the rest of the class as much as possible. Which was a lot, thanks to the help of Mrs. Heatherhort. I was Mrs. Heath's best reader and she adored me.

She said, "Teach, I know you're probably busy, but can I pull Maly for a while?"

I glanced at my teacher in acceptance and she agreed with a wave of her hand. Mrs. Heath could steal me for three whole hours.

She brought me to the locked up, closed down library. Books lay on the floor, bookshelves tipped over and boxes torn. What a mess. With all the last minute book drop-offs and the library aides busy attending last day parties, the library took on a life of chaos.

But I had a blast. Mrs. Heath was awesome. She wasn't as quiet as she looked - face it, she's a librarian. She played loud religious music. The vice principal, Mr. Lee, scowled at us until he was louder than the music. She kept on like she didn't hear him and he finally just turned on his heels and left - slamming the door behind him.

I had read all the novels in the library so every time I picked one up we'd talk about it like "That was the best book ever!" Or "It was okay, not the best for a Newberry Honor Book, though" on and on and on until noon. I still had another hour with her but we had to take our lunch break.

I slowly walked into the noisy cafeteria which could be heard from down the hall. Everyone at one table was trying to speak louder than all the other tables. It was a zoo.

The lunch ladies served the "mystery" pot pie that they served every holiday or special occasion. I don't know why 'cause it gave Jim food poisoning. I never touch the stuff, just sort of ate around it.

After the rowdy lunch was over I spent my last hour with Mrs. Heath. I always wondered why she had bruises every day. I asked her once and she said, "I'm just so clumsy...:"

"Oh, okay," I had replied softly, almost sorry I asked the question because she seemed bothered after that. But I never brought it up again.

I went to my homeroom class and it was ballistic. Paper airplanes soared overhead with notes like "Start the count down in two minutes" or "Summer" or "Come to my house" and more. I could have sworn the room was hopping and about to fall apart until..... Rrrr rrrriiiiiiiiiiiiiinnnnnnnnnnggggggggg!!!!!!!!!!

Everyone screamed and shouted almost at the same time "School's Out!!!" It was a struggle just to get out the front door to old familiar Route 12.

On the way home, I thought about how I'd spend my summer. I knew I'd work at The Pig Grocery Store for .50 an hour, 50 hours a month, three months (all summer except on weekends and only for one hour on slow days and two hours on fast ones). The job paid okay. At least a good one for a kid. I worked there every summer. My family needed the money and the customers needed the groceries.

I got to Berry Lane and, of course, Mrs. W was on her porch with three tall glasses of lemonade.

"You like Kate?"

"Oh doll, she's just like a real daughter, everythin' I imagined."

"I'm glad. Do you know where she is?"

"In the kitchen. Help her will ya hun?"

"Sure."

I walked into her silent kitchen and there was Kate in the same dress as before, but this time washed and stitched.

"Hey, Peanut B.P.!"

"Did you go to school today?"

"With everyone looking for me, I wouldn't be surprised if they found me HERE," Kate said anxiously.

"They can't, Mrs. W would be stunned, angry and arrested. Do you want that to happen?"

"Nah, don't guess so."

"Okay then, put on a good face and deal with it 'k?"

"Like I said, I like you, so - FINE," Kate said, the last bit with sarcasm.

I went home, ate supper and drifted to bed. Been a long day... Be a long morn' too.

Chapter 7

I woke up at 5:00 in the morning. I did my same morning routine as if I was going to Mrs. W's. But today is Wednesday, so off to 'The Pig'. I looked at myself, satisfied with what I saw. In the summer I spent more time in the morning, just to get fresh. And putting my bouncy curls into that small gap in the back of my favorite cap took skill.

Mrs. Gruent was already there. She owned the place.

"Hi P.B. Patty."

Everyone had their own way of calling me by my nickname. I had names for them too.

"Hello, Mrs. G. Many deliveries today?"

"Only two sweet."

"Who to?"

"Mrs. Heatherhort and Ms. Kimberly."

"Sure thing."

"Oh, and hun, get an early start. I need you to man the register too. Of course I'll pay extra, my little helper."

"Oh, you're real sweet, Mrs. G."

"But just for you, all the others don't work as hard."

"Got it."

"Hurry off."

I grabbed The Pig's delivery bike and rode to Ms. Kimberly's house first. She's dating the milkman, Mr. Cole. I knocked. Mr. C. opened the door. He spends most of his time there.

"Hello Mal Pat." (see, everyone has a nickname for me).

"Hello Mr. Cole. I have a delivery for Ms. Kimberly."

"Oh, well, I'll be glad to give it to her." He pulled out some wrinkled bills and put them in my hand.

"Do you need change, Mr. Cole?"

"No, thanks, keep it. Save up for something."

"Okay, thanks again."

He shut the red door behind me.

I pulled up the bike and headed for Mrs. Heath's house. I traveled down a dirt and gravel road, to a small bluish, gray house.

A big man opened the door and yelled to a shadow inside, "Some kid. Get here now!" His voice was raspy and tough. The shadow dropped everything and scrambled to the door, wiping her hands on her apron.

"Mrs. Heath?" I asked stunned.

"Is something the matter child?" She stood, not for very long till....

"Um, delivery," slipped through my open mouth.

"Oh, that's grand, thank you." She took out some money and "snuck" two quarters into my hand and said real soft, "Keep the extra."

"Thanks very much Mrs. Heath!"

As I walked down the porch steps I looked back and saw Mrs. Heath getting scolded by her husband.

He said, "Why'd you give that good for nothing girl extra?"

She stuttered and he, he....... slapped her. She covered her face and fell into the porch swing. Tears streamed down her face.

33

My heart was racing at the fact he had the nerve! I wanted to go back and help her. But I could end up the same way so I just quickly got on the bike and rode on, shaking.

When I pulled up to the store, an old Ford was parked in front of it. Mrs. G was reading a fashion magazine. Nobody in this town had fashion any'who. I waved and opened the second register out of four. And waited.

Chapter 8

As I waited, I thought of poor Mrs. Heath. No one but me knew. What should I do for her? I wondered until Sam Frenchez walked up to me and threw all his groceries on the side table while I calculated it.

I wondered what the most popular person in my grade was doing in front of me.

I said, "Did you run out of milk at the castle? Or on your way to a party I wasn't invited to?"

"Ha, ha," he replied. "Why do I have to have a reason? And plus, I like it here, you?"

"Uh, I work here. So why ARE you here?"

"Heard a rumor they needed someone to run the register - that's me! Say 'hi' to your new work buddy!" he said with a chuckle.

"You, work? That is funny!"

"No foolin', really."

I thought, this could be disastrous, "But, but, you, here?"

"Yeah, well catch ya later, Mal PB Pat."

I felt some weird bubbly feeling inside. I felt it all of a sudden.

I asked Mrs. G, "You hire any new workers?"

"Just that precious boy, Sam."

"Yeah, sure, precious," I mumbled softly.

"You say something?"

"No, I didn't. I'll be out working now, okay?"

"Sure, carry on."

I spent thirty more minutes in there. It was a fast day. Sixteen custos (customers). For a city with a population of 207, that's good.

I ran down Berry Lane still bubbling with random thoughts and awkward feelings from the store that puzzled me. I turned onto Mrs. W's porch. She was pale and looked as if she was unable to breathe.

I got up to her and she was making gagging noises, like gasps.

"Mrs. W, can you breath?" I didn't get a response, just a noise.

I ran toward the kitchen phone and the operator picked up.

"Please tell me your issue and location as fast and calmly as possible."

Gosh, someone's choking and they want me to be calm, I thought.

"My neighbor is unable to breathe. I'm at 1264 Berry Lane. Send a car fast, she is turning red!!" I screamed to the operator.

"A car is on it's way. Stay Calm. Thank you." replied the operator like a robot.

I looked around and noticed Kate on the couch.

"Kate!!" I said with a very mad, impatient voice.

"What, can't I rest P.B.P?"

"No, not when Mrs. W's choking. You're in charge. You're 'spose to help her, not kill her!!! By that time my voice was yelling.

She sat there and said, "You're the one who put me with her."

"Well, I at least did you a favor. What'd you feed her?"

"Honey oats, that's all."

"Honey? Honey? She's allergic to honey, deathly allergic!"

"I'm sorry, I really am," She started crying.

I felt bad for yelling at her. She didn't know, my heart started beating again when she hugged me and we heard sirens wailing.

Chapter 9

Just as Mrs. W , Kate and I got to the hospital, the doctor put all the questions on me.

"I am Dr. Rathbond. Does the patient have any allergies?" He stared, waiting impatiently for the answer.

"Um, yes, honey."

"Okay, who will pay for the patient's visit?"

I didn't think, I just said, "We will figure it out, don't worry, you'll get your money."

He got snobby at me after that comment so I did back. I hated the way he called her a "patient".

Kate was freaking out, "P.B.P, what are we gonna do? I don't know where I can stay." She was almost to the point of tears.

"It'll be alright. I'll figure something out."
I looked around. "Dr. Rathbond, is there a
way for Mrs. White's daughter," I shot a glance
at Kate when I said 'daughter', "to maybe stay
with and assist the nurses, you know, keep her
company?"

He shot me a dart, like a 'stop making
things so hard look' and said, "I'll see."

When he turned away, Kate said in a whisper,
"You're a lifesaver, thanks."

I walked back home. I still had work in the
morning.

———

Chapter 10

I got up really slow the next morning. Worrying is not for kids, I decided. I was just pulling my curls through my hat when I saw Sam walking up the drive.

"Hi, Queen of the Curls."

"At least you're in the presence of royalty."

"I figured since we work together might as well walk together," he explained.

"I already have to see you more than I would like," I said. And we both gave a laughing sigh.

The rest of the walk was pretty quiet. When we got to the store, Mrs. G was there. She waved for us to hurry up. We started trotting.

When we got to her she said, "Six deliveries. Pieces (Sam's nickname) help her out will ya?"

I was thinking, now I have to see him even longer.

Before I could say anything, he said, "Sure, what folks need the goods?"

"Ms Sandy, Mrs. Evens, Mr. Perry,"

My face lit up at the sound of my grand-dad, "Mr. Cole, Mrs. Nelly and Tifany, you know Tifany, don't you?"

"Yes," we both replied.

We left The Pig on our way to Mr. Perry's, my granddad.

"This is my granddad's house," I said as we walked up to a brick house.

"Really?"

"I don't get to see him too much, but he's really funny. You two would make a pair."

"Wow, I finally get a compliment!"

"That was a statement, not a compliment," I responded.

"Well, I count it as a half compliment."

"Fine, I don't care."

Then a deep voice broke in, "What ya'll youngsters doin'?"

"Hi Pops, how's it been? You need to come see us some time."

"Alright," Pops replied, " I guess you got my green tomatoes?"

"Sure do," Sam broke in. He reached out his hand to shake my granddad's like a grownup and introduced himself. "Sam Franchez, nice to meet you."

"Well, Sam ole boy, you got your hands full today." Pop shot a glance at me.

I added, "Or the other way around."

I shot Pops a smile and waved goodbye as we left to deliver the rest of the groceries. The other people were the regular boring ones.

———

Chapter 11

Back at the store it looked as if the whole town was there. People were hammered against the walls with cameras.

Then, I saw her.

A lady, very slim, in a red dress. She looked vaguely familiar - she looked like the lady on the cover of the fashion magazine Mrs. G was reading the other day.

"Who is that?" Sam asked with excitement.

"Like I'd know. I don't know any famous people."

The strangest thing happened just then.

The lady walked right up to me and said, "Darling, I'm back!" She grabbed my hand

and tugged at it. I backed away, not knowing what to do.

Finally, she let go and glided out of the store followed by all the cameras and people. She waved back at the crowd, got into her shiny car and drove off.

"Sure you don't know her?" Sam asked.

"I don't," I argued.

People were trying to actually talk to me then. But to their disappointment I didn't have a clue. Mrs. G. closed down The Pig for the rest of the day because of the lady.

I made my way home, puzzled about the lady and tired from all the events of the night before. As I made my way toward my house, the lady's car was parked in the drive. I opened the screen door and saw three pairs of eyes staring at me. One of them was the lady's. I stood, not moving. I was stunned, frozen, mouth wide open until a bit of water formed in the left corner of it.

Mom had a bit of tears in her eyes. Choking on tears she said, "Pack your bags."

"Why?"

The lady broke in, "Maly, I'm Geneva....," she stood smiling, "Your Mom."

"How? Why?" I stammered.

"Come on Mal, we're going to California! Get all your clothes!" The lady smiled, excited at the thought of leaving.

Chapter 12

Everything suddenly made sense. That day I saw the suitcases in the hallway and thought we were moving or going on a trip. The sealed note. It was all to tell me I was a foster kid. The lady would have come to get me sooner but then I got sick. I didn't want it to make sense. I wasn't one to give up without a fight and I was sure I wouldn't be going with that lady. Why didn't "Mom" stop her. Can't she do anything about this?

I was walking up the stairs like I had done a thousand times. Except this time was stomach churning, different. I turned half way around just to see three blurs through my tears. I didn't know what to do. Mom wasn't Mom, that meant Dad wasn't Dad and Pops wasn't Pops either.

I pulled out an old tattered suitcase and threw in five pairs of shorts, four jeans and seven shirts. I grabbed my bag with jello arms, took one look at my old room and quietly shut the door.

I wrapped my arms around the two people I'd been living with for as long as I can remember and squeezed with all my might.

Then, I estimated about the distance from the lady and the door and ran past her pushing all my strength forward. It was a good plan to begin with, but where was I going to stop? I'm one of the fastest people in the county. Second fastest in my school to be exact. But even I can't run forever.

Every puff of air that entered or left my body was a sound of hate and disgust except for a few filled with fear and anger. My heart was like a step, thump, thump, thump like it was in a race with my legs. I turned the corner and a pair of arms caught me.

I struggled to get free until I looked up and into the green eyes of Pops as he said, "I'm sorry."

I couldn't believe it. "But, what , hu?"

"Listen Maly, things have a way of working out so just go with it. They're looking for you everywhere so let's go inside. I have something I want you to see."

I stepped through the entryway into his small home and saw a journal on the square table where he ate his meals. It was small and red.

I turned the page and it was filled with sayings passed down from his family. First, there was a name, then the saying. I skimmed over them and they seemed to have a soothing effect on me, like my life was going perfect.

I saw the name "James Erle Perry" at the top of a page with his saying underneath. "Life's ocean will take hold, but it's up to you to swim or sink in the great sea."

I stared at the page and whispered, "Wow, this really helps, thanks Pops."

He smiled, "I made a bed for you upstairs..."

Before he could finish his sentence I blurted out, "Pops, how did you know I'd come?"

He gave me his old familiar grin and said, "I had a feeling you'd end up here."

I walked down the narrow hall, up the stairs and turned into a room with a bed, side table and dresser.

"Maly, you can't stay forever but when you're ready just go because you'll know better than anyone."

I thought about what he had just said and let it sink into my head. When would I be ready? I lay on the small bed thinking.

After a while, I got up and wrote him a letter that read:

"I know you said I'd know better than anyone and so I think I'm ready to take on this new adventure. I'm not going to say that I like it. Before I got here with you, if you were to ask me if I was ready I'd have said no. But your little red book with its sayings - well, I guess life is taking hold of me so I best swim. There is no better person to thank than you. Thanks for everything."

I folded the paper and set it at his door because when he awoke I'd be gone.

Chapter 13

I got in the car while Geneva put my suitcase in the trunk. I looked back with tear
filled eyes as the car drove off. Pops must have
known 'cause he was on the porch wiping tears
away with the back of his hand. I let out a
little wave as I rode by, leaving him behind in
the dust.

The only people I didn't get to say goodbye to was Mrs. W and Kate. I hoped they
would be okay. They had to be okay. I just
about jumped out of the car. I didn't though.
Everything, my town, my "family," me, gone.

I slept for most of the ride, which was pretty
far. The days melted together. I found myself
with streams of water running down my face

every time I woke up. I'd cry myself back to sleep again hoping when I awoke things would be like they were yesterday. But after waking up the third time, in the car, with Geneva, I decided there was really nothing I could do about my life right now. I dozed back to sleep, too tired to cry anymore.

I woke up when "Mom" yelled, "Darling, you'll love all the red carpets, Hollywood premiers, photo shoots, and my job. You'll love my job!"

I looked around and the first thing that caught my eye was staggered letters that read "HOLLYWOOD" in white. We were riding down a red bricked street with a line of palm trees on both sides of our car. People were riding past in flashy cars and looking every bit the part I always thought this place would be like.

We pulled up to a very big, clean, brick mansion. It looked bigger than every house on Berry Lane put together.

She said with satisfaction, "Here we are!"

Chapter 14

I almost cursed by accident, filled with excitement at the thought that this place was home. But it also triggered in my mind the fact that I was gone from The Pig, gone from my "family," gone from Sam (which I didn't mind that much) and gone from all I knew, just.....gone.

I came up to the steps and opened the heavy wooden door that stood between me and my new life. I stepped in with torn dirty Converses onto the white marble floors and right in front of me was a winding staircase covered in red carpet.

I must have looked shocked 'cause Mom said, "Isn't it wonderful? This isn't even the best part!!!"

She signaled me to come with her. She turned the knob on a little white door and stepped back so I could go in. Out in front of me was a crystal blue pool. The biggest one I had ever seen. The water looked like glass because the wind back there was just perfectly still.

Mom said, "Doll, what do you think about that!"

I wanted to say I don't care, take me back. But I said instead, "Wow! Where is my room?"

She led me up the twisted staircase and through a little door was a room. My room. It was the most beautiful thing I'd ever seen. A light colored wood loft bed six feet high, a little desk, a gray couch under the bed and shelves filled with books beside it. There were also shelves on the other side of the room.

"The shelves have pull out compartments for clothes," Mom explained. She waved her hand to the far side of the room and said, "There's your bathroom and walk in closet. Come find me when you put your clothes away. I'm going to get you a new pair of shoes and some new clothes at a couple of shops I know in town."

I didn't care about the clothes I wore. Almost anything looked great on my athletic body, tan complexion and curly blackish hair. And that was the first thing Mom noticed about me.

"Oh my gracious! People would give everything for a body and skin tone like yours!!! It's to die for!"

"Thanks."

At every store we went (which was more than two), Mom was greeted by name. And no one failed to comment on how beautiful I was. No one had ever commented on how pretty I was at school. They just picked on me... was that their way of showing they were jealous? If they could only see me now. The populars would turn green with envy and their heads would spin.

People from the shops carried all our bags for us from one store to the next. It was like everyone was one big shopping family and all Mom had to say was, "Put it on my tab."

All of sudden she looked at me and at her watch, quickly turned to the salesperson helping us and said, "Claire, pick out a shirt and shorts for Maly, quickly - I have to go down to the studio and I don't know where the time went!"

Chapter 15

On command, Claire swiftly went into action while her assistant led me to the dressing room. In two minutes flat, I was out of my old clothes, transformed into part of the Hollywood scene. Claire took a look at my curls tied tightly in a ponytail in the back. She unraveled my ribbon and brushed my hair out. Claire stepped back and said, "Now, that's more like it!"

Mom nodded her approval and we were off in a whirlwind of shopping bags and perfume. Mom pulled my arm and started running for the car.

"What ssttuuuddiooo?" my voice trailed off as she ran.

I wish I had never gone to the studio. They put me in a little room and a lady poked at my head and body till I was sore. Then she threw some clothes on me that looked very expensive and yelled in a rough voice, "You look beautiful, now move along kid." I was super lucky I didn't have to see her again after that.

A tall man walked in wearing a black suit. He looked handsome, but definitely not for me. He had to be at least thirty years older than me. He grabbed my mom's hand and put his wet slobbery lips against it. She chuckled, but it gave me a funny tingling feeling that started at my toes up to my neck. He was about to kiss her until I waved an annoyed, "I'm here wave". Mom caught up.

"This is my beautiful daughter, Molly, Maggy…"

"Maly, remember?" I chimed in.

"Yeah, Maly." It looked as if she was melting into his grayish brownish eyes.

I had to talk for myself, "Mom brought me here to audition, or something - to be a model?"

"Oh, yes, well…" Mom grabbed his shoulder before he could finish and whispered something in his ear. His face lit up and he said, "You've got the part! And may I comment on your beautiful complexion."

I knew the trick, I gave him a dirty look that slapped the smile off his face.

He said, "Your mother can teach you all about the runway."

I nodded. "Super," I said in a peppy way and moved my fist to my hip.

Mom talked about the man (David) all the way home. It made me want to throw up 'cause she added so many weird details. I let her talk, it wasn't like he would be my dad or anything.

That was true until one night....

Chapter 16

I was on the very top of my bed when a gray car pulled up with a shadowy figure in it... David of course. He was wearing a suit, almost the same as a tux. And Mom looked breathtaking in her sparkly night blue dress that hugged to every curve of her body and released a slit at the neck like a V. He lead her into the open door of his car and rode off leaving me and the house full of servants in his dust trail. I'm glad he's gone.

Mom woke me up by the sound of a door opening. She had just gotten home and it was 5:30 in the morning. I felt as if I had been left out, alone.... Forgotten. So what, I've dealt with worse. I just lay in bed thinking, doing nothing but thinking.

I dreamed of back "home" and I wished I could spend my birthday there. I wasn't even gonna mention it, even though it was today.

I opened my eyes, stared out into the open, and daydreamed like I was in my own little part of the world. My place, a place to think. I rolled over onto my back and saw a quick quiver of movement. Just my imagination I thought. I saw a white gown pop up in front of me and it held up a brand new outfit. It looked gorgeous. But one thing was wrong with it, it didn't look like me.

"Surprise," Mom said as she handed me the outfit with one hand. Her other hand was behind her back.

"Mom, what's behind your back?"

She tried to put my question off. "Do you like your outfit? You'll be modeling it on Saturday!" She noticed my eyes were trying to curve around her body - she finally held out a thick book." "This was mine when I was thirteen, I know you're twelve, but I'm sure you'll love it!"

"Thank you, it is all so... wonderful." My voice got a little shaky. I wasn't a very good liar.

"Put the dress on, I'll show you how to model it," She said with a twinkle in her eyes.

Once I shut my bathroom door I took one good look at it. It was a turquoise blue dress with white trim at the top and white straps. From a little above the waist it was crinkled which made it beautiful.

I stepped in it and noticed that the bottom swayed loosely and the top crinkles fit like elastic to my smallish curved chest. I took my hair down from my ponytail and noticed that like everything, it was very pretty on me. It didn't look like something I'd wear but, very pretty. I came out and gave a twirl like I'd seen Mom do.

She clapped, "You are my baby!"

We went through about an hour of walking, twirling and face expressions. Mom had a catwalk built in the pool house with mirrors all around so you could take an honest look at how you were doing.

People back home would have laughed at the idea of a little country girl, a model... and I still had a hard time believing it, yet here I was.

Chapter 17

I had been with Mom for more than a year. My life was modeling jobs, private tutors, clothes and special events. By now I was pretty sick and tired of the whole Hollywood idea. But I had to stick it out for Mom. It was her life. And the money. She loved money and what it could buy. Everything I made went into my own bank account - for college she said. I wondered if she didn't have a lot of it growing up. At least that way we were both the same. Not having much but having enough. Now she had more than enough and she wanted to share it with her daughter. I wondered if she loved money more than even me.

I was to be in a fashion show for a major designer tonight. My Mom said it would be a huge step in my career. We rode in a very fancy car to a building that could hold more than the population from my old town. It was huge. There were glass doors and black marble floors with huge rugs that had fancy patterns.

Mom had to show her I.D. and a special card from the agency about me and they let us through. I walked backstage and saw a giant platform. The catwalk that unfolded in front of me which ended in a blur of lights looked so much bigger than any I had ever seen. My stomach tightened into a ball and it rolled around inside my belly.

I wasn't about to do this… before I could even disagree, I pulled my hand out of my Mom's and ran. I pressed my hands to the sides of my dress so it wouldn't fly up. I rammed the back exit door and threw myself out into the wet streets.

I ran and ran. It gave me a feeling like I owned the world.

The cold drops of water mixed with the thrashing winds made the rain seem like needles hitting my face and arms. I looked both ways, but no shelter until I came upon a little brick law office. I remembered the book Mom had given me. The name on the book was the same as the sign on the law office.

I ran up the stairs, water splashing on top of my feet. I knocked on the door. A little old lady in a dull pink, plaid dress opened the door and took one look.

"Oh my, child, come in, come in. Take a seat, I'll get you a towel."

I nodded and tried to get some words out of my mouth but my lips wouldn't move.

She came back with two white towels.

"Now, what happened, from the beginning?" she gently asked.

"I was with my Mom, she practically forced me to model at the show today. I didn't want to so I ran," the words spilled out.

"Your Mom reminds me of me when I had my girl. I always wanted her to earn an easy living. Honey she's beautiful, even though I barely remember her because she doesn't call or come by," the old lady whispered.

Then she looked at me and said, "You look like her, but a cuter, more wholesome version. Do you play sports? Of course you do, you have an athlete's body. What's your Mom's name?"

"Geneva" I replied.

She almost burst into tears as she grabbed me and my face was thrust against her chest.

"My baby, my baby," she whispered over and over.

"What?" I looked up puzzled.

"You're my grandbaby."

I felt proud once again to have a grandparent. This was sort of awkward, but calming too. She smelled great, of lavender and the valley just after a big rain storm.

"Can I move in with you Gran?" I asked.

"Why? You don't like it with your Mother?"

"Well, I'm not used to it and ….."

"Sure honey, I know. Your Mom, she is still learning and young. We can move you in tomorrow. But for now, please discuss this with your mother."

"Okay, thanks Gran!"

Chapter 18

After I had run off, Gran called my Mom and explained everything. She must have done a good job because when Mom picked me up she didn't yell or anything. On the way home she explained to me that I was born when she was young and she wasn't married. She knew she couldn't raise me by herself and she was too proud to stay with Gran and "be a burden". So she put me into foster care and headed for California. She vowed she would come back. And she did. I loved her for wanting the best for me. Even now, as she said ok to my plans to move in with Gran.

We loaded up the two trucks with all the stuff Mom had bought me. I felt bad walking out on her. But I would still see her, just not all the time. And no more modeling. Besides, she had David. When I thought about that, I didn't feel so bad any more.

I got in a black SUV next to Gran and took one good look at Mom. She smiled and waved. She knew it was the right thing to do. But it was the first time in a long time that I had thought about home and the people I missed.

Gran's house wasn't as big as Mom's but still very huge. She had Delores who helped her with the cleaning and the cooking. I thought Gran's place looked better than Mom's. Not so sophisticated I guess. I loved it there. And I loved Gran. But the more I thought about it, the more I missed my old town.

"Hey, Gran," I asked her one day when we were sitting on the back porch sipping fresh squeezed lemonade, "Do you like the country?"

She looked at me funny.

"I know it's a weird question. Would you mind moving there and maybe...starting a business?"

"Why, I love the country. But economically it isn't the best place for businesses."

I looked sad but she went on, "But honey, I want the best, happiest life for you after all you've already faced. No father, foster parents and a not so great real Mom."

"Gran, you are the most thoughtful and caring person!" I exclaimed as I jumped up to hug her neck, "I think this move will mean more to me than the world!"

She smiled, "I'm glad you think so. I'm ready to retire and I've always fantasized about moving to the country."

So, in just two months, Gran rounded up a new house in Alabama, sold her other one and retired. She taught me it's not about fame, fortune or the city. Instead it's about the people you share your life with.

My whole life got restored, all thanks to Gran. Now, I don't have to spend my summer at The Pig, delivering groceries with that showboat Sam. But I choose to. And I don't have to go to school at a public school, but I want to. And no one told me I had to go to Mrs. W's funeral or Kate's adoption day, but

I decided to. So my life is just the way I've always dreamed of.

"Hey Peanut Butter Patty, help your old Gran in here will ya?"

Well, I could do without the dish washing duty.

Author's Note:

I hope you enjoyed reading my first book as much as I enjoyed filling it's pages with my thoughts and inspiration.

With your parent's permission, email me at pbpatty@akwablueproductions.com. I'll send you my quarterly newsletter called "Sparkle" and you'll get a sneak peek into my latest book, <u>3 Blocks Down the Street</u>. You can also learn fun stuff like the word of the day and meet me and my friends as we pal around.

3173512

Made in the USA